THE SUBLIME

THE SUBLIME

poems
by Jonathan Holden

Winner, Vassar Miller Prize in Poetry
Yusef Komunyakaa, Judge

University of North Texas Press
Denton, Texas

First Edition 1996

10 9 8 7 6 5 4 3 2 1

Permissions:
University of North Texas Press
P.O. Box 13856
Denton, TX 76203

The paper used in this book meets the minimum requirements of the American
National Standard for Permanence of Paper for Printed Library Materials,
z39.48.1984. Binding materials have been
chosen for durability.

Library of Congress Cataloging-in-Publication Data

Holden, Jonathan.
    The sublime / by Jonathan Holden.
        p.   cm.
    ISBN 1-57441-020-2
    I. Title.
    PS3558.034775S83   1996
    811'.54—dc20   96-14748
                                                            CIP

Design by Amy Layton

ACKNOWLEDGMENTS

The following poems have appeared or are scheduled to appear in the following places:

"Dry-Wall" and "Zeno's Paradox" in *Beloit Poetry Journal*; "Pope's House" in *The Kenyon Review*; "Sea World" in *Many Mountains Moving*; "The Principle of Duality" and "School Yard" in *Missouri Review*; "Gulf," "Spook House" and "Western Meadowlark" in *New Delta Review*; "Gould" in *The New England Review*; "December Sunset" in *New Letters*; "Old Newsreel Footage" in *New York Quarterly*; "After Closing Luigi Cremona's *Projective Geometry*," "Night Game" and "The Third Party" in *Poetry*; "Teaching My Son to Drive" in *Poet and Critic*; "Divorce" in *River Styx*; "Love in the Time of Cholera" in *The Southern Review*; "Emptying the House" and "The Model Train" in *Tar River Poetry Review*; "Faking" in *The Spoon River Poetry Review*; "Three Mile Island" in *Stone Country*; "Grown Men Shooting Baskets" in *Texas Review*.

TABLE OF CONTENTS

I. KNOWING

II. OLD NEWSREEL FOOTAGE

III. EARTHSHINE

I. KNOWING

I say: a flower! and out of the oblivion into which
my voice consigns every outline, apart from the known
calyxes, there arises musically, the delicate idea itself,
the flower absent from all bouquets.
                            —Stephane Mallarme

i.
There are two ways of doing everything:
talking, making music, making love.
One is human. To err is human. The violinist
sweats. Maybe, like Glenn Gould on the keyboard
he sings along. Gould hummed so loud
he can be heard
on the master tapes. Maybe he groans.
The violin requires
strength. One's shoulder starts to hurt,
cramp up. I remember, in the middle
of a weekday morning making love
a cramp blinking on, a light-bulb
burning in my right calf
like a screaming newborn
exacting my attention.
No choice except to climb out of bed
and stand on my right leg
and bear down
to try to placate it,
then go back to bed,
recover the warm lining

of the dream that we'd been in,
breathing closely
on the coals, hoping
they will blush and blink
back to life,
that before one p.m.,
when we would have to
pull our clothes back on and drive to work,
we could create a condition
so like music we would be able
to take it with us secretly
like a melody, say the opening
of Bach's *Die Kunst Der Fugue*
right at the knot which the viola
like a caught breath, almost a sob,
ties as it begins to overlap
the second violin
which, though praising God,
has become the tide, seems
already to be grieving steadily.

ii.
Glenn Gould last publicly performed
on April 10, 1964. He wrote
The presence of the audience
is impossible to reconcile
with the essentially private act
of music-making,
that music was best served
by the recording studio,
by any medium which permits one
the luxury of second-guessing
the interpretive decision.

From then on, like the Princess and the pea,
unable to play when the piano bench
might be a sixteenth of an inch
too high,
he thought as Stephane Mallarme, who wrote
In the pure work the poet
disappears, yields his place to the words
taking light from mutual reflection—
like an actual train of fire over precious stones
replacing the human direction
of the phrase.
It is not from basic sonorities
made by brass and strings and woodwind
that music will emerge in clarity.

iii.
I'm not sure when it was
I began to understand
the world's orders to us are inherently
contradictory. That to be adult
well is to live naively, to live
as though you didn't know you're going to die,
make love to cramped ecstatic paradox.
Johann Sebastian Bach,
whose music Gould liked best, Gould,
the purist, could still praise as
valuable for its humanity.
All that time, until he died at fifty
he'd been singing along,
human in spite of himself.
I remember singing Bach, in choirs.
Hearing the other parts was like standing
within the structure of a thunderhead,

glimpsing from the corner of an eye
flesh-tones of sunlight catching
on a furling cornice
while the graying roofs below
keep tumbling, and you're being
buoyed by this updraft
out of yourself, drawing
breath to sing, human, helpless, knowing
hardly knowing what you're doing.

Aiming into a slate sky
the twin-engined fuselage of my son's
Winchester pump shot-gun,
as I wait to pull the trigger
to take off again, I am surprised
at how good this feels.
Is it an acquired taste?
I feel like a geometry teacher
holding a heavy pointer in my arms,
though I'm not teaching him. He's
teaching me. *Pull.*
He wings a forehand out over the corn-stalks.
I follow it with my pointer, seeking
a proof, some evidence
of cause-and-effect. The clay pigeon
hesitates. I pull the trigger, the gun butts
my shoulder with a BOW! The disk stalls
subsides back into the field. Missed.
So far I'm two for ten. Zack's turn.
He opened the breach, releasing smoky wind,
a salty pecan taste of cordite.
One by one we add a row of shells
like a train of yellow freight cars, thumb them home.
Pull. I fling a forehand out. BOW, the pigeon's
powdered. *Pull.* Fling. Powdered. Fling. Powdered.
I like it when my son does anything
better than I do. That's a father's job.

But now a crescent-shaped formation of gulls is coming.
They curve over us, Zack following. BOW!
One gull breaks formation, is descending,
its wing hanging open, a page of yesterday's
newspaper. It settles like a bedsheet
only as far away as second base.
Zack blasts at it. Debris splatters just short
of the pin. He blasts again. Short of the pin.
The gull is watching us, unblinking.
Why don't we just go up and kill it, I suggest.
I'm hoping to sound casual. I sound tired.
The gull's still watching us as we approach
like two golfers, businesslike. Two martians.
One shot flattens its face and neck
into a dusty scrap, eyeless,
a ripped sock. *What
are we doing?* Killing humans
is an acquired taste, I guess.
But this?

KNOWING

i.

My son, at eight, would want to save the life
of the plate-eyed deer mouse
the cat occasionally carried home
to tutor for an afternoon.
She'd drop it on the rug, and sock it in the head
till it felt sick and wanted to go home
and wobbled up to the teacher to ask, "Please?
I don't feel well. May I go home?"
but the teacher smiled, "Stop being a sissy,"
and swiped it in the head
until the new pupil was bewildered,
felt sicker in the stomach,
and would've cried except it was too scared,
and the teacher was talking. "Run!" "Stop!"
"Sit down!" "Raise your hand!"
"Shit in your pants!" "Run!"
"Sit down!" "Limp!" "That's it!"
"Break a leg!" "Run!" "That's it!"
"Break your neck!" "Run!"
"Throw up!" "That's it!" She would
encourage it, ration out its hope
till it could be stored
beneath the sofa like a toy
and be counted on to cooperate.
In half an hour it would be released
like a little old man from the hospital.
Gamely, totteringly, he'll venture from cover
out into the light, offer himself again,
hoping that school is over.

ii.
Go! The children lined along the sidelines
are shrieking in a way they'd never
shriek over arithmetic
as the differences between fast and slow
widen and grow   until it's glaring
as a scream, a public obscenity—
All men are not created equal—
the truth we must pretend we cannot see,
don't even know about, even
as it's being repeated   louder until
the winners burst lightly through the tape
and are already banking gracefully away
to accept their ribbons
as if they'd known the outcome in advance.

iii.
The man and the woman love
to talk when they're making love,
though not all the time.
Sometimes they'll let themselves die
by drowning. Sometimes
they'll watch themselves drown. They don't need
any equipment. No mirrors. Only some words.
A code. Protection from spies.
Mmm! Sweetcorn! Equipment,
they laugh, is for the birds,
for the bourgeoisie.
The rest don't know.
They take things—an arm, a shoulder—
literally. Sometimes, during their deaths
and rebirths, the man and the woman
like to watch themselves

as they do it. *As if our bodies*
were a couple of puppies,
she sighs. They marvel:
how the more they do it the more
deeply they love each other.
Then they laugh about how naive
was the boys' belief
that "strange" is attractive, about how
the more deeply they come
to understand the art
of familiarity, the faster
it snowballs, the more they know
the more they want more love.
And the more they know, the more
they know what they know
what they know
of love.

TEACHING MY SON TO DRIVE

The Wareham Cemetery seems the safest place,
a miniature town of children's blocks,
a place so harmless
the baby rabbit squatting in the drive
doesn't know enough
to move. We're alone.
The only policemen on duty are trees
holding over us the shelter of their quiet.
I climb out. My son
sets our phone book on my seat,
gets in my place, sits down, releases
the brake, shifts into first, lets out
the clutch. The car jerks and stammers,
fighting off a stroke, totters forward,
and we're creaking like a toy train up its track
in this toy world, we're a joke.
Slow is comic when it's slow enough.
We crawl around the loop
past the little buildings without doors,
my son peering over the wheel,
his face grim,
determined not to stall, pretending
to steer the enormous thing
that's steering him.

SPOOK HOUSE

At the door to what he'd heard
so much about, my son,
at eight years, hesitates.
Then to the girl at the gate
he submits a freckled hand.
She stamps it, his fingers
curl hard around my thumb,
and he tows me forward,
we are fending our way
through the yowling, pulsing air
into a room where, lit
dimly by a red bulb
we find ourselves surrounded
by the dingy contraptions of Hell—
a dummy hung like a sack
from the ceiling, embalmed corpses
that on cue, sit
bolt up and glare at you.
We blunder through a door.
We're in the hall.
He releases my thumb
and marches grimly away,
offers the girl his hand,
ducks into the underworld
again, reappears unscathed
in the hall, marches around
for another tour of hell,
reappears, and goes around
again, as if to make sure
whatever was there is gone,

as if he were practicing
the restlessness that is male,
an urge that can't refrain
from exploring any dark place,
but must poke at it until
like a dead animal
it doesn't move anymore,
all the shadows are cleared
away and, he can't help it,
he's bored, he can't think
what to do with himself
except go somewhere else,
anywhere he has not gone before,
where there is a new darkness.

THE THIRD PARTY

Her mind
was so much more than she—
it was a third party.
Like some large instrument
at the love-bed,
it made an exotic guest: able
to decide on its own
whether or not to participate.

Hurt people bear with them
a slightly puzzled look,
a scar between the eyes
where their grief is lodged,
a lead plummet.
I'd seen her, a scientist, delve
into a differential
equation like a boy rudely
unlocking an orange by
forcing the seams from the lobes
to spring it open.
But as she analyzed her rotten marriage
she was plain stupid.

There is no one, I think,
whose private life isn't more
or less unlovely than daily weather.
It's the country where our friends
all speak the same tongue.
Whatever you do,
every angle of the bones,

has been tried before.
and the speech of grief,
a dead end in itself,
so satisfying, so useless,
is the same tautology, the last
cliché, the one area of expertise
in which, sooner or later,
we get as good as anybody.

As she talked, her hand on mine,
heavy, opaque, and sad,
her heartbeat a mute syllable
typed out in code,
her beautiful mind—so
much better than she—could no more
save her than the pure
scaffolding of chamber music
as it goes up
can save the four, short
scholarly men huddled under it,
a quartet of carpenters
with too much on their hands,
measuring, filing, conferring
like mad to assemble
another section of an intelligence
almost too plausible.

Like a calculated smile, it,
too, might break
a man's heart or save
his life,
but is, indeed, heartless,
better than we are,
hardly any help at all.

II. OLD NEWSREEL FOOTAGE

> Ah, love, let us be true
> To one another!
> —Matthew Arnold

And didn't our love seem almost a political act,
to turn away from the footage of the F-15s
following each other in single file
along a slow assembly-line as if on parade,
toy after toy, each copy being lifted, smoking
off the scorched belt, then the next
and the next being mass-produced into an industrial sky.
As we kissed, and kissed more deeply, trying
to make the picture go away, to deny this, I saw
that what we had been watching, what so fascinated us
was only another kind of factory, that it was inevitable
the activity we call "war" be conducted in round-the-clock shifts,
that military bases and state penitentiaries
are designed to manufacture identical deaths
as heartlessly as a commercial egg factory
where the lights are kept on to get the hens
to produce eggs faster than is natural. The men
all in the same sand-and-spinach uniform
were as similar as hens. Even the General strutting
like a fat rooster had donned those funny pajamas
like a surgeon's gown, a carpenter's apron—
what boys wear when they put on
the frightening costumes of efficiency,
roll up their sleeves and get ready to get down
to business, to be men. Wasn't it Spengler
who said it takes about twenty years for hens to forget,

for a generation to be bred ignorant of the shop floor,
enough time for new men who,
because they don't know any better, are willing
to put on the killing pajamas, the aprons again
and, like their grandfathers, earnestly go to work?
Isn't it twenty years since I used to watch, rapt,
with field glasses, the fleas circling
the hive of Alameda Naval Air Station,
the carrier like a slate, shelved landform
that would appear overnight, a grey grandmother,
to babysit the skyline for a week,
then go back to work in Asia. Ah, Love,
didn't it seem subversive to turn off the t.v.,
how we followed each other wordless, deep
into the immediate truth of the next kiss.
And the next. And decided then and there
we would take our costumes off for the afternoon,
we would not go to work that day
or the next. Or the next.

—for Ana

SEA WORLD, SAN DIEGO, CALIFORNIA

> Notice Neptune, though,
> Taming a sea horse . . .
>> —Robert Browning, "My Last Duchess"

In the same eye-hurting thalo-blue
of every high school pool,
caught in its quaking network of light,
I sit, polite and cowed, watching
a formation of dolphins bank, submerge
leap in unison, coaxed
by the kind of jaunty crewcut guy
I used to envy in high school, perhaps still
envy, watching him fling
a cheerleader up and catch her—
Whee! an American word, the word
at the top of the charts.
All the boys here are athletes, and the girls too.
But the best athletes are the dolphins.
Sleek and intent, they're obliging as servants.
The first dolphin, Bunny, does a barrel-roll
through a day-glo hoop. Spatter of applause.
Then it's Bob's turn. Next goes Nancy,
as Bunny comes sidling over to our side
to receive a present, like a communion wafer.
She smirks gratefully up at a sinewy girl
who tosses out a snootful of herring
like a handful of peanuts and chips, it's
Party Time. Bunny returns to her place in line
to wait, knowing that the beach-ball trick
is next, if she can only balance the ball

long enough and be a good sport,
one of the teachers will flip out more chips.
She thinks she's chosen this life,
that she's choosing right now
to roll under again and rise
on cue into the blue brilliance
as when a prisoner decides
to tattle on his fellow cell-mates to earn
an extra Big-Mac and fries
and maybe even a cold beer in his cell—
he's come to count on that beer,
the one cold beer of the day,
and an extra cigarette,
when he can compose himself,
enjoy a moment of reflection
to contemplate the inner life—
a moment of what he believes
is pleasure.

OLD NEWSREEL FOOTAGE

"like cockroaches scurrying for cover when you
turn on the kitchen light"
                    —an Air Force pilot describing Iraqui troops
                        during Desert Storm

If our grandfathers could only
see themselves, important
as penguins, all buttoned up
in their black tails,
they'd either have to cringe
in shame or else
to laugh so hard they'd almost
wet their pants. Their Great War
would never have occurred.

But look at them!
How could they have known any better?
They'd hardly even learned properly
to walk! Each step they tried
broke into this rapid, nervous
little waddle. Hindenberg
was silly. A fat puppet
in costume. Wind up the key
sticking out its back and it would totter
forward like a two-year-old slightly
out of kilter, bow,
frown sententiously, then,
with a cute rat-a-tat-tat,
pump the hand of another diplomat.

And there they go again, waddling
straight ahead in quick staccato.
New rows of infantry are flopping
out of trenches like geese
startling behind stick and falling,
flopping out and falling, more
are flopping out and struggling
and falling, flopping, playing dead.
They knew next to nothing
about the history they had thought
to make, it's over.
And now another tickertape parade.

THREE MILE ISLAND

A raw, thin drizzle wets
the fuses of the trees
as I turn with my dog down 17th Street.
It's the first day
of April—too cold, still,
for the forsythia to catch.
The light rain seeps
down as it should.
And all around me this reassurance,
small business as usual,
yackety-yak of the jays
over who gets what. Sparrows
too sure of the world
to worry, peck at the ground,
get lucky and spurt away.
Squirrels fuss, little current
events flicking the curls
of their tails. And my own children,
grinding their coloring books, indoors all
morning practicing new syllables.
The corner of Leavenworth and 17th
is deserted, no news
except the flashing yellow signal
reciting its lone word—
slow, slow—moistening the skin
of the intersection yellow.
The streets are evacuated for now.
It is Sunday.

LOVE IN THE TIME OF CHOLERA

Those of us who have grown addicted
to long, long-distance sighs,
static-filled gaps over a telephone
can still remember
the re-enactable, lingering potency
of the old-fashioned *billet doux.*
They understand fully the difference
between "Dear" _____ and "Dearest."
Tearing a letter open, they have experienced
the vertiginous chasm between
the polite, equivocal "Yours"
and the naked "Your,"
the vulgarity of "Darling." They know
how in *Amor en El Tiempo del Colera*
Ferdinando wins Fermina with letters,
how singlemindedly, like Don Quixote,
he invents his own romance—
that *Amor*, at its truest, like a book
sets its words down tremblingly
faithfully in cursive,
that it is when one is struggling
like a bee fallen in the bathtub
to keep afloat, stay eye-level
with the surface, in order
to see where he is
that a man will resort to the clichés
I love you, I adore you—
desperate shorthand for matters
too incendiary to be touched
except by an adequate music,

by a poetry capable of breathing
life into the grey coal
of even the lowliest syllable.
Laboring, up late, alone
on a letter answering a letter,
retracing tenderly as if
by fingertip its tentative words,
retracing a word   and retracing it,
at times, they are startled by a bee-sting.
Though in pain themselves, instead
of groaning, they chuckle privately, pitying
those poor souls who may never
possess the world enough,
for whom love ended with the telephone.

TAKING ROCKY'S FATHER TO THE HOSPITAL

I first saw him in the sudden light
in his pajamas, trying to comprehend us
through drizzled eyes, a good 250 pounds
of athlete, tyrant, king and cocksman
gone to seed—this grizzled, bearded guy
who, for all the times they told him to his face,
refused to hear that he was going to die.

"Father, you are going to the hospital."
Rocky framed each word with the same
too-loud, too careful and too bland phrasing
you'd use to get through to some simpleton.
That is how you speak to a man
through his brain tumor.
The old man muttered something ornery.

We gave him our shoulders, inched him
toward the door. He knew what was coming
off enough to hate our help, and in the doorway
balked, mumbled something his daughter
instantly understood, she grabbed a cup
and pulled his penis out, until the trickle
stopped and we started forward again.
Somehow we got him in the car.

I had forgotten this is what hospitals
were for. Busy as a bus terminal, but cleaner.
We wheeled him along the waxed hall,
up one wing to the small bright room
where we would wait until his bus came in.

Stood around while the night nurse hung
his robe. She kept up this bright chatter
as she helped him to bed, when I saw
for the first time the back of his head,
all soft and bubbly where they'd first cut in.
He started to whimper about being lonely
tonight. The nurse chattered on, pretending
she didn't know exactly what he meant.

We didn't mention it on the way to the car.
I found myself studying the floor.
I couldn't make my eyes meet Rocky's anymore
for all the loathing which as yet
he hardly knew was there.

DRY-WALL

Those great, gray sandwiches
that come taped back-
to-back look buoyant until you edge
your shoulder under one and
hoist. The weight's a corpse.
Every wobble in it makes you weak.
If you flip its gray belly up
too fast, its skin cracks
along this wrinkled fault, the cardboard
bows, it buckles up the middle.
The stuff chips like stale bread.
The slab's a mummy made of chalk,
a birthday cake wrapped up
in bandages. It can't tense back
to clench a nail with sap,
it's just make up, it's rhetoric,
the cheap way to cover a mistake—
the edges of those studs you splintered,
those nails whose necks you broke,
then crucified in rage.
Everything you do is a cover-up—
the joists, each post, the flue,
even the whiskery grain of rough-cut beams
boxed in—as though anybody thought
you could deny such facts
or the fact that we have bones
that break or that the lines deepening
in your face are who you are.

THE MODEL TRAIN

"This is the saddest story I ever heard."
—*The Good Soldier*, by Ford Maddox Ford

As D. put it to me in the bar, sadly,
That life ended, or began to, on the day
when, by flying stand-by, he got home
five hours earlier than planned
to find a yellow van blocking the driveway.
It was late March but mild,
a characterless Sunday afternoon,
a diluted sunlight glistening in the front yard's
muddy patches. No one, not even the dog
came out the front door to greet him.
Where were his two kids? I'll never be sure why,
he said, but instead of barging in the front door
he found himself going around back,
approaching it discreetly to peek in.
Whether what he found, then, was what he half
expected—almost wanted—to find or not
he'll never, he confessed, be all that sure.
He found his wife motionless
on the living room floor,
curled up for comfort in the arms
of an old friend. Her eyes were closed
as if she were a child asleep.
What shocked him most, she wore a look
he'd never seen on her before, she looked
calm, blissfully content.
The man, a family friend, was the kind
he knew she'd always gravitated toward

before—a local politician, well to do,
an older man with reassuring shoulders.
As Bertrand Russell was to Lady Ottoline,
he was the latest in a line of men.

"This one," he said to her, tremblingly calm,
"is the straw that broke the camel's back,"
conscious that he hadn't said "could break,"
remembering the things his friends who'd been
through a divorce had said. "You don't know
what you're getting into, you can't know."
"You mean it's like an acid trip," he'd laughed.
They shook their heads a little sadly.
Younger than he was, they seemed older.
"You just don't know."
But he remembered watching
our closest mountain friends, the Logans,
Jan and Jim, divorce.
Like me, it had made him furious.
She'd been the one to take what amounted
to a wrecking bar not just to their
lives but to the lives of all their friends.
So many events, like things, being shoveled
into black plastic bags and trucked off to the dump.
Intimacy comes down to history. I know this.
But history, we agreed, when its exoskeleton
has been revealed,
when it doesn't have a story anymore,
is unwieldy as a corpse,
just things, and nearly impossible to budge.
It takes a moving van.

Together we recalled the Logans' twins.
For a year Jan and Jim had existed without sleep
How every night the boys took turns
sitting up suddenly to scream and wake the other.
(Anyone dragged bodily out of the warm
lining of a dream knows how deep that violation is.)
They took turns snoozing in the car, so as not to hear.
That winter had been particularly cruel.
To kick week after week against
the cold for over half the year,
keeping warm by friction, gets you sullen.
I remember Jan's prim face
refined with exhaustion, the thin whine
like a metal file that undercut her voice.
How when she'd bundle the twins and groceries
in with the snow and set them on the rug
the boys would study you with a cold,
sullen curiosity, their blue eyes
so sober and so wide that when
they both studied you together, the sea
had come into the room, inhuman force.
The future itself was sitting on the rug,
Humorless, it was waiting to be fed.
It didn't care what the hell you wanted.

Thing by thing, they'd heaped up everything
which in retrospect sums up a life.
Jan wanted animals. Two nondescript
gray cats moved in, then a black lab,

Jovinian, an easy-going slob. A dozen hens
were hobbling around, glaring at the dirt.
A platoon of geese were marching
on that foul parade ground, making mean remarks.
Three goats, all faintly smiling, occupied
the new shop where Jim's radial-arm saw
presided over concrete and flies.
Two years passed. Jan's voice was hearty.
She could now ruefully recount the nights
when both boys were screaming, and she,
spanking them hopelessly to sleep, would see
her small hand close into a fist.
The boys were three. Revving, charging behind trucks,
turning goat-turds over in their hands,
checking the name of every object to be sure
that grass was still called grass today,
fighting the pedals of their bikes
or racing back to the bench in tears,
they'd permeated the place.

Passion—it's like clutching in each hand
a fistful of powdered magnesium.
Someone's touched it with a match. It sputters
and starts to flash so brilliantly, you have
to squint, the fragments spit and spark
in all directions. What you feel
is panic, but you're anaesthetized
with fascination, in a state of shock.
You've lost both hands. You're helpless.
You don't know it. All you can do is blink
surprised. You think you're in control.
Which means you're not.

D. could only half remember, he confessed,
the times he'd been in love outside of marriage.
Sexual passion is quite a lot like pain,
real only as long as it is real,
you don't believe in it until it's real.
We both remembered being furious at Jan
but for selfish reasons.
When two couples in their twenties are close friends
they use each other for company, to compare notes about
new jobs, bad bosses, tips on house repairs.
I remember huddling with them simply for warmth
on January nights, 8,000 ft., nights so cold
under your boots the snow would squawk.
We had these marathon Monopoly games,
it took a grammar as blunt as those bright city blocks
to warm you up—hopping happily past
the pink-faced cop with the whistle in his yap
saying GO TO JAIL, one hop over Luxury Tax
spang on Boardwalk.
The stove was warm. And the game,
The game was a way to keep warm.

I believe one reason
why the divorce rate is so high
in California is because
in that climate people need each other
less. There's no necessity.
People are either a nuisance or a sport.
But in the Front Range, winter
starts before Thanksgiving. Even in June
we'd sometimes get three feet of snow
like wet cement. Summer for two months.

Late August, when it finally comes, is like dry mead.
It's potent, an infection, it goes straight to the head.
You can't seem to touch anything enough.
It makes one desperate.
I'm trying to imagine the fatal supper.
Jan had just got home
from a weekend raft-trip down the Arkansas,
leaving Jim at home to tend the twins.
She's aglow with the otherness of sun,
the foreign country that is moving water.
Jim's glad to see her. He senses
this rapt softness in his wife,
as if she owns a secret so delicate
it could spoil if exposed to the air too rudely.
What the words were to the ensuing scene
we have to guess. Suppose Jim asked what the matter was.
Almost dreamily, as if she were doing him
a favor to share the revelation, she replies
that she can now see how dreary marriage is.
She begins to recite, deliberately
in a histrionic voice, her list of reasons.
It's a speech she's been working on for years.

The nightmare of real life is starker
and far more banal than we'd thought.
We stare straight at the world. We stare
and stare. We stare. There's not a shred of myth.
D. is staring at me, dry-eyed
in the bar. His voice is hoarse.

He begins to recite, deliberately, his list.
From that day, he says, we began systematically
to take apart our life, like an HO-gauge
model train set. Detail by detail, we disassembled it—
the plastic tunnels, the tiny cottages
fit to scale, the model, too-green hills
with their plastic sheep, the miniature
river pumped by batteries, that trickled
through the idyllic town, as phony
as a Swiss chalet, the smiling plastic cows,
the tiny trees, the fake clouds,
the fake river which, if you bent down
close and squinted and tried to put
yourself inside the scenery,
was almost real.

DIVORCE

The musical notes retain their original pitch
but the instruments ruin them.
Clang comes out as *clank,*
ding-dong as *dink-donk,*
pink the hue of *puke,*
bang reduced to *bung*
reduced to *bonk*
reduced to *bank.*
Honey to *money.*

EMPTYING THE HOUSE

Driving the thin county road
determinedly numb
along the north edge of the swamp,
passing gray, ramshackle woods,
passing Dudleys', passing Garrities'
I come to a low stone wall, turn in
and unlock the back porch door.

The original, wide-boarded floors,
unoccupied now, lie open,
a map of routes as regular as the weather,
traces fading as deer traces in a field,
a trace leading from cupboard to table,
another from dining room to kitchen—
the kitchen still arranged as if expecting company,
a shiny body without a heart.

I just sit, unable
to begin disassembling a world left so intact,
remembering when we used to come
barging through the back door on holidays
how broad our shoulders were,
they filled the narrow hall,
our bulk bruised the place,
floors quaked under our heavy boots.
Wherever we tramped
the upstairs would seem to give
as we shook the walls to make sure
they were there, stalking
from window to window to check

how the sycamore was set
and finally even such details as where
the old sunlight stretched on the kitchen floor.
I sit and look.   And look.
To move would be to bump into a void.

All morning the rooms grow cooler, quieter
as the house settles more deeply
into itself,
a concerto whose volume is gradually fading,
an ocean liner sinking.
I conduct it downward.
Outdoors the trees are slippery
in the weak sun. Wild geese
pass low over the roof
in the same old raucous wedges.
Still, in the back yard, the giant sycamore
with all its kinks and creaking knots
presides, holding the lawn, the peeling
garage and the goldfish pond together
as if it had custody of the place.

At length, I'm ready to rise
from my lethargy and begin the job,
to hurl once and for all
my single weight
into the literal tons
of junk which, taken together, amount
to a facsimile of actual life.
None of it is alive.
I talk to myself and the boards, I talk
in order to keep moving
like a child repeating to himself his parents' instructions:

In the cold you must never,
no matter how tired you think
you are, never sit down in the snow.
I talk to distract myself,
to drown the woo of inertia,
its whisper: *Go on, feel sorry for yourself.*
Sit down. It's only reasonable
not to move anymore. Sit down
and listen. Sit here
and sorrow. Listen.

It was by touching the world,
by physically seizing whatever was left
that I managed to get moving again,
by handling in the hall closet my mother's coats
(garments that seemed still to burn
with a shallow warmth of their own)
that I freed myself of their weight.
By touching shyly those of my father's books
I'd determined to take away.
It was by lifting between
both palms the cheeks of a ceramic lamp,
by fingering clean socks
all folded and aimed in their drawers.
For me, childhood will never again
be a literal country.

Now, whenever I try to imagine the house
not somewhere to the east,
I float, queasy as a compass needle
without magnetic north,

And I know why I used to like the snow.
How it would free the front lawn from the curb
and let it blend into the street,
shortening the low stone wall
until the front yard was anonymous
and I had lost all sense of direction,
I was lightfooted, I could stand
unburdened in the new world
where I own nothing
because we all, owning the snow,
the white, the everything
again are on familiar ground.

DECEMBER SUNSET

This last soft lie. Almost
inaudible. A tenderness.
This lingering look. Ambiguous.
As if beckoning us. The road
already lonely. The birch trees
flushed. Fierce. All facing
west. Waiting. In suspense.
A few lucky twigs. Still
blessed. A few shingles
grazed. A faintest
remembrance of kisses across
the barn roof. Sighs
of light over the sleek
drifts. A few wisps of it
left. A breath of it.
Along the fence rail, this last
rare whisper. And less. And
less.   And less . . .

III. EARTHSHINE

EARTHSHINE

I used to study from the back seat
the rate at which the roadside trees went striding
past the hazy distant trees.
The hazier a tree
the deeper the distance where it stood.
The ghostliest, scarcely discernible
across the field, didn't move
at all, but like a line
of spectators, would
turn their heads together
toward us as if to watch us pass
before mist erased them.
I didn't know the calculus, but knew
there had to be a way
to forecast the position
of each tree in relation
to every other tree
continuously.

On a clear night
sometimes I could almost swear I'd seen
the rings of Saturn through my binoculars.
They were famous. In *Pictorial Astronomy*
I pored over photographs of Saturn: ˙
Saturn in the nude as if reclining
on one elbow, rings blurred,
sumptuous as the purr of a plump cat.
Saturn at attention, severe, rings edge on
almost invisible. I memorized
its postures the way I studied

the faces of the stars in *Photoplay*,
Sports Illustrated or on the screen.
But I can remember my disappointment
at seeing the great
Yankee southpaw Whitey Ford
alive. He looked like my dentist.

In *Pictorial Astronomy* we read
that a planet didn't twinkle like a star,
that Mars could be distinguished
by its reddish cast.
I scoured, re-scoured the sky for a stale star
that might be red. Was Mars inhabited?
It was conjectured
that its faint markings
could be a system of canals.
That was the year of the earliest
little league kiss I ever had.
I remember launching out, down
toward Sally's face, this planet
like a crescent moon turning
toward me, becoming
full, I was landing
on the surface.
Frankness of raw skin.
A shock to see, on television,
after the Mars landing, only what we'd known
we'd find. No canals. No hint of red.
Just rocks. And rocks.
Rocks: the surface
of the world:
our own.

One clear winter afternoon
I noticed that around
the crescent moon there was
a memory of moon:
the word for moon:
a faint presentiment
of moon: an eclipse?
But then my neighbors must
have noticed it. Why
wasn't this strange moon in the news?
Was there a name for it?
Before I knew the word
I knew there was.

Miss Griswold had taught us in third grade
the righthand way to read: forward.
But how to read backward too
wasn't taught in grade school.
Or the ambidextrous way.
To single out a gang of stars.
To learn they were The Pleiades,
which *sounded* like a constellation:
a tinkling of piano notes
dim dimly dimming *Pleiades.*
To glimpse earthshine: Read
backward and forward
at the same time.

SCHOOL YARD

The cries of the children in the school yard
score the noon sun like stray
gears, tooth to teeth, the voices
of gears loose in the larger
immaculate machine of day revolving
toward its sense of destination,
declining on oils of cold slick sunlight
down the track that is its routine,
as ignorant as a wheel
passing over this brief space,
the wheel feeling only
the constant single point
to which it is tangent,
the reassuring pressure of where
it is, the closest thing
to pleasure it will ever know.

But the children do not feel it
as the wheel passes over.
They leap and spill around
each other like springy little cogs,
unattached to this work. It is we,
our bodies silent as if disconnected,
who know that the wheel's circumference
is tall as the bridges that the wind destroys
as our weather comes clear, goes hard.
It is we whose skin is instinct
for the direction in which the work

tends, as if gravity could roll
from under our feet
to the blue furnaces on the edge
of the horizon.

We try our presence
against that possibility, the wheel's
arrival, the rim bearing on us
in its ignorance, joining
us to all the other points
that are the one point the wheel
is certain of,
while in the dead center of the day
the children cry in the school yard
and the bare trees outside
suck their shadows into themselves
as we do and wait,
subsumed in the routine.

GROWN MEN SHOOTING BASKETS

It is all they ever wanted to do—
with a slight flex of knees to entrust
the ball to another arc,
to send up these theories—
a vocation they will never outgrow.
And watching them circle the glass backboard,
how their gazes yearn toward it,
I remember the hours when, like them, I studied
alone in the driveway,
longingly gauging the rim, solving
the same problem over again,
completing the thought of a jumpshot
from the top of the key,
an idea finer than the sagging garage
or ninth-grade social studies.
You could fill the vacant pages on the afternoon
with beautiful zeroes.
The right answer was like a perfect dive—
near silence. The diver slips under
the pool shuts with a click.
Solemn now, deep in contemplation,
they circle, shoot and shoot and shoot,
preparing for nothing, doing
the only homework they ever loved.

KARATE

Mel Brown was teaching us
logic: First soften your opponent.
Seize the hair like a housewife
snapping lint from a rug and
snap. Or break one arm, blind him
with the splinters of his own
nose and so make him available
for the greater mechanical advantage
of both your elbows,
the next link in an argument
leading straight to the mat.
        Mel checked us again.
A welterweight, he was forged
like a wedge, perfect.
On the glistening basalt of his chest
your fist could break.

        Daintily
as some finicky high-
fashion photographer coaxing
a girl's surly chin,
cajoling, tilting her head by
fingertip to hold a pose,
he retouched our stances, adjusted
my knee, my drooping
elbows, the tickling flatteries
of his attentions pleasant
as the fussings of a barber.

        Satisfied, he stepped
back. He was, as that saying goes,
undressing us with his eyes,
he was snapping
our pictures.

ZENO'S PARADOX

That absence of imagination sprang
from fear which for years let any man
who swung an axe do the impossible—
clobber the log he aimed at every time.
Even though the axe-head had always
half the distance to the log to go,
it would negotiate this space,
manage somehow to flatten the packed
differentials that remained. It was
a wonder a body could walk across
his room and touch the wall when,
logically, a moving arrow didn't move
at all. But because we're a little
braver than Zeno was, we now know why:
We can face infinity.
When I start out upon this sunlit
floor to cross the room, I'll never
fail. With each stride I take
I perform a commonplace—straddle
the infinite—I cross the infinite
to reach the kitchen wall.

AFTER CLOSING LUIGI CREMONA'S *PROJECTIVE GEOMETRY*

I don't know how the clouds out here
survived. Points are so perfect that
if you believe in them enough
they prick. Each point will leave
a tiny bruise. And lines are sharp.
The pure ones cut you like the starched
edges of grass-blades, it smarts,
though the wound's too fine to see.
In bristles, they can nearly chafe you
raw. Even here, outdoors, as I stagger
and blink, swamped in this hot mess
of light and sticky shadow, that black
and white headache won't go away.
The points cling in stains, I can't
get rid of them. The vestige
of a line is running furtively along
the street. And the letter *A prime*
still glows in the midst of the elm
tree, while the Principle of Duality
has just flown up and alighted
with those sparrows on the wires.
I can hardly walk, it's underwater,
it's all a jungle here. The leaves flash
their bellies, swimming and wriggling
along in unison, they gobble everything.
The best-trimmed lawns glitter
with chaos like smashed glass. The light's
like acid. You can feel it working
mildly on your skin. The more acid
in the light the more I like it.

I'm going to take a bath in it, splash
this stuff up into my eyes and rub
until the swelling goes away,
then dive in over my head and soak
myself for as long as it takes
to make the dazzle of the last hard
point dissolve in space.

INTEGRALS

Erect, arched in disdain,
the integrals drift from left
across white windless pages
to the right,
serene as swans.
        Tall,
beautiful seen from afar
on the wavering water, each
curves with the balanced severity
of a fine tool weighed in the palm.

       Gaining energy now, they
break into a canter—stallions
bobbing the great crests of their manes.
No one suspects their power
who has not seen them rampage.
          Like bulldozers, they build
by adding
      dirt to dirt to stumps added
      to boulders to broken glass added
      to live trees by the roots added
to hillsides, to whole
housing developments
         that roll, foaming before them,
the tumbling end of a broken wave
in one mangled sum: dandelions, old
beer-cans and broken
windows—gravestones all
rolled into one.

Yes, with the use of tables
integration is as easy as that:
the mere squeeze of a trigger, no
second thought. The swans
cannot feel the pain
it happens so fast.

POPE'S HOUSE

Everything goes like clockwork in Pope's house.
Outdoors, I watch a ridge go up in smoke.
In here, it's calm. Everything's methodical.
There's not a sound. I've never seen lumber
milled as mercilessly as this. The couplets
are like good boards, they mate, they're pressed
that tight, sanded down and varnished
to a sheen. This is a puzzle in which each
piece is made the same—lined up like pews—
in which they click together, tongue-in-groove.
It's dull. There's nothing dangerous
to do. The clock's so loud you'd like to break the
clock, and yet you can't. Somehow
there's always something there that holds you
back. You might, in the afternoon, make
a modest, perfunctory kind of love; it would be
functional. But even if you were capable
of passion or did you dare let a curse fly;
should you despair or yell or hit somebody
or merely disturb the position of a chair
you would soon regret it. The butler would be
there, ready to restore the furniture back
to its proper order and to turn on you the same
fixed smile that angels have as they defend,
with their long boat-hooks and their boots,
the parlor of the saved; he would be ready
to reason with you. It wouldn't matter,
then, how hard you pleaded that you couldn't
help it—that seeing the snow blow off
that mountain was like seeing it burn.

He would prove to you that your seeing was
wrong, he would have all the answers.
You'd shrink under his logic like a dog.
There would be no whining. He wouldn't stop
until your silence said that you had finally
come to all the same conclusions he had,
and he was satisfied you were ashamed.

THE PRINCIPLE OF DUALITY

Three sparrows shivering in three trees
make a floor so pure
they can't catch it with their claws,
they scratch at it.

*

With this knife, three
grand slices of the sunset
make one target of a seed
too hard to peck.

*

Sparrows don't worry
about duality.
They jab once, twice,
then spurt away. They're lucky.

*

The harder Hawthorne stared
the surer he was
he could detect something infernal
behind old Goodie's catechizing smile.
Was it lava or cold mud?
The thing befuddled him.

*

Suppose you and your lover have just
perfected a technique to meter pleasure
so minutely to the edge of pain
you can't even remember what you screamed.
Shower briskly. Then shut up
and eat. Don't talk too much.
Don't look at anything too long.

NIGHT GAME

The infielders are definite
as sparrows at work.
Split that seed with one peck
or starve.
There is no minor league
for birds. There is
exactly one way
to pirouette into a double play
perfectly. The birds
don't dare reflect on what
they do, each hop, each stab and
scramble through the air into the
catch of the sycamore's
top twigs
is a necessity,
absolute. To stay alive
out in the field, you be
an authority on parabolas
and fear philosophy.

FAKING

Watching my daughter inclining
to her flute in grade school band,
I remember straining to keep
my handhold in that creaking,
wheezing junkyard of bad sound
until I'd fallen behind,
I could hear the band going
on parting like water
in a brook around
a rock—me—and closing
loudly beyond while I waited
left behind, listening
in a kind of vertigo
(What if I get caught?)
almost as lonely as the time
years later, I found myself
on the cliff's face, slinging
a hammer to set pitons, listening
to the rock: *tink, tink, tink?*
attending to how each blow should register
a half-tone higher,
my very being attuned
to three true tones, questioning
the rock. A three-word question:
Three: blind: mice?
Then ascending a half-
step to set the next one
and listening, relying

on music, calling it
to account, being
called—*Three: blind: mice?*
to account, vowing
once again, never
to lie again.

Through the open car window
seven needles in a haystack
BoPEEP-doodle-our-PEOple!
snatched by ear out of the moving
prairie, like you
already fading, passed, gone.
BoPEEP-doodle-our-PEOple!
If I could find it, it would be
points of sunlight glancing
off a brooch so near shades
of gold in these moving
grasses I could scarcely distinguish
it from the grasses. Like you
it is always gone.

BoPEEP-doodle-our-PEO-ple!
The bird pulled it off like a string
of catches on this flying
trapeze which keeps swinging
back. If birds' songs simply mean
I'm here! I'm here!
then why a song so baroque?
How many notes did it have?
Which notes were extra?

In the Beatles' "Blackbird"
you can hear a meadowlark, its song
canned as the slow-motion replay
of a pass-reception on TV:
Love studied into pornography,

Bo-PEEP-diddle-diddle-her-PEEP-hole!
The bird falls off a see-saw,
hesitates, picks itself
back up on the rising board,
completes its song.
It does it again.

I prefer the song that eludes me,
this one which we are passing,
banjo music picked out
through wind and distance
already falling behind

gone and not gone.

—for Ana

THE SUBLIME

Tell me, Jim, have you read Heidegger?
You're a professional weatherman.
That means we're both phenomenologists
like him. We study and forecast things
that we perceive. I once dismissed him
as a crank. I found it ludicrous
the big question he would ask
and ask again: *Wherein*
is the ground of Being,
until one day, six months ago,
on this breezy April afternoon
I encountered a weather that I'd heard
about but hadn't ever seen first hand.
A kind of front (a secret one) encroached
from the northwest—a front
of nothingness
all along my left side.

My first thought was "tumor,"
but a CAT scan saw nothing. I submitted
to an MRI. And there it was.
On an illuminated screen, the neurologist
fit a dozen black and white transparencies.
How like the contact sheets they were
from snapshots of the earth, filmed
from our nightly weather satellite.
There were the outlines of both hemispheres.
Those white spots, he explained,
which look like the radar blips of thunderstorms
were lesions.

It was the classic profile of M.S.
Except for the numbness,
I did not feel ill.
Yet I *was* ill,
theoretically.

Jim, I used to think that "The Sublime"
was what Wordsworth meant
when he said he'd been "fostered alike
by beauty and by fear."
He talked about Nature as his mother:
"Her." He glimpsed Her in the landscape.
She frightened him.
Or it was the kind of pleasant vertigo
an English lord might feel
as a spectator at the park overlook
beholding The Matterhorn
or studying from a museum bench
a painting of The Matterhorn.
I remember rafting on the Arkansas
outside of Salida. Sometimes, as the raft
dove off a rock shelf and I was staring up
at a mountain range about
to crash on me, I knew
I was about to die
and yet I wasn't
really going to,
and knew
that later I would recollect it
with a delicious shudder.

This was different.
As I studied the pictures
of the landscape taken from orbit
after orbit over my own inner weather
I marvelled at the time-lapse
between the forecast on the screen
and my fate. If there were any horror
it was at how *little* emotion I could feel.
This was knowledge I had no use for.
I remembered a friend who,
though at risk for AIDS, decided
quite rationally to forego
having his blood tested for H.I.V.
reasoning that if he tested positive
he would not want to know.
My fate was equally
theoretical.
This is the modern Sublime, Jim.
It is fear
made theoretical.
It's as if you were a spectator
to some one else's personal disaster
on t.v.

Jim, though I'm a weatherman,
and, of course, I *do* know better
scientifically,
it seems I'm still inclined
like a romantic
to read the weather in my mood.

I remember when a cold front would come through,
magnificent and final, the night sky
jibbering with light, constantly
jumping and answering, signalling
madly to itself like Lear.
I know it's sentimental.
But now, simply remembering
that way to be afraid
when I was a child,
when I thought that one could hide
inside the covers
is comforting,
as if there were a place anywhere
inside or outside
to hide from this,
some place.